Walt Disney's
Snow White
and the SEVEN DWARFS

Cover illustration by Don Williams

 A Golden

Copyright © 1999, 2003 Disney Enterprises, Inc. Al[...] n Copyright
Conventions. Published in the United States by Gol[...] oks, a division
of Random House, Inc., New York, and simultar[...] d, Toronto.
Originally published by Golden Books in 1999. Go[...] G colophon,
and the distinctive gold spine are [...]
Library of Congress Control Number [...]
ISBN: 0-7364-2186-6
www.randomhouse.com/kids/disney
www.goldenbooks.com
Printed in the United States of America   10 9 8 7 6 5 4 3 2

Long ago, in a faraway kingdom, there lived a lovely young princess named Snow White.

Her stepmother, the Queen, was cruel and
vain. She hated anyone whose beauty rivaled her
own—and she watched her stepdaughter with
angry, jealous eyes.

The Queen had magic powers and owned a wondrous mirror that spoke. Every day she stood before it and asked:

"Magic Mirror on the wall,
Who is the fairest one of all?"

And every day the mirror answered:

"You are the fairest one of all, O Queen,
The fairest our eyes have ever seen."

As time passed, Snow White grew more and more beautiful—and the Queen grew more and more envious. So she forced the princess to dress in rags and work from dawn to dusk.

Despite all the hard work, Snow White stayed sweet, gentle, and cheerful.

Day after day she washed and swept and scrubbed. And day after day she dreamed of a handsome prince who would come and carry her off to his castle.

One day when the Queen spoke to her mirror, it replied with the news she had been dreading. There was now someone even more beautiful than the Queen. And that person was Snow White!

The Queen sent for her huntsman.

"Take Snow White deep into the forest," she said, "and there, my faithful huntsman, you will kill her."

The man begged the Queen to have mercy, but she would not be persuaded. "Silence!" she warned. "You know the penalty if you fail!"

The next day Snow White, never suspecting that she was in danger, went off with the Huntsman.

When they were deep in the woods, the Huntsman drew his knife. Then, suddenly, he fell to his knees.

"I can't do it," he sobbed. "Forgive me." He told her it was the Queen who had ordered this wicked deed.

"The Queen?" gasped Snow White.

"She's jealous of you," said the Huntsman. "She'll stop at nothing. Quick—run away and don't come back. I'll lie to the Queen. Now, go! Run! Hide!"

Frightened, Snow White fled through the woods. Branches tore at her clothes. Sharp twigs scratched her arms and legs. Strange eyes stared from the shadows. Danger lurked everywhere. Snow White ran on and on.

At last Snow White fell wearily to the ground and began to weep. The gentle animals of the forest gathered around and tried to comfort her. Chirping and chattering, they led her to a tiny cottage.

"Oh," said Snow White, "it's adorable! Just like a doll's house."

But inside, the little tables and chairs were covered with dust, and the sink was filled with dirty dishes.

"My!" said Snow White. "Perhaps the children who live here are orphans and need someone to take care of them. Maybe they'll let me stay and keep house for them."

The animals all helped, and soon the place was neat and tidy.

Meanwhile, the Seven Dwarfs, who lived in the cottage, were heading home from the mine, where they worked.

The Dwarfs were amazed to find their house
so clean. They were even more amazed when they
went upstairs and saw Snow White!

"It's a girl!" said Doc.

"She's beautiful," sighed Bashful.

"Aw!" said Grumpy. "She's going to be trouble!
Mark my words!"

Snow White woke with a start and saw the
Dwarfs gathered around her. "Why, you're not
children," she said. "You're little men!"

"I read your names on the beds," she continued.
"Let me guess who you are. You're Doc. And you're
Bashful. You're Sleepy. You're Sneezy. And you're
Happy and Dopey. And you must be Grumpy!"

When Snow White told the Dwarfs about
the Queen's plan to kill her, they decided that she
should stay with them.

"We're askin' for trouble," huffed Grumpy.

"But we can't let her get caught by that kwicked
ween—I mean, wicked queen!" said Doc. The
others agreed.

That night after supper, they all sang and
danced and made merry music. Bashful played the
concertina. Happy tapped the drums. Sleepy tooted
his horn. Grumpy played the organ. And Dopey
wiggled his ears!

Snow White loved her new friends. And she felt
safe at last.

Meanwhile, the Queen had learned from her mirror that Snow White was still alive.

With a magic spell, she turned herself into an old peddler woman. She filled a basket with apples, putting a poisoned apple on top. "One bite," she cackled, "and Snow White will sleep forever. Then I'll be the fairest in the land!"

The next morning before they left for the mine, the Dwarfs warned Snow White to be on her guard.

"Don't let nobody or nothin' in the house," said Grumpy.

"Oh, Grumpy," said Snow White, "you *do* care! I'll be careful, I promise." She kissed him and the others good-bye, and the Dwarfs went cheerfully off to work.

A few minutes later, the Queen came to
the kitchen window.

"Making pies, dearie?" she asked. "It's apple pies
the men love. Here, taste one of these." She held
the poisoned apple out to Snow White.

Snow White remembered the Dwarfs' warning.
But the woman looked harmless, and the apple
looked delicious.

Snow White bit the apple. Then, with a sigh,
she fell to the floor.

Told by the birds and animals that something was wrong, the Dwarfs raced back to the cottage. They saw the Queen sneaking off, and they ran after her.

As storm clouds gathered and rain began to fall, the Dwarfs chased the Queen to the top of a high, rocky mountain.

Crack! There was a flash of lightning, and the evil queen fell to her doom below.

But it was too late for Snow White. She was so
beautiful, even in death, that the Dwarfs could not
bear to part with her. They built her a coffin of
glass and gold, and day and night they kept watch
over their beloved princess.

One day a handsome prince came riding
through the forest. As soon as he saw Snow White,
he fell in love with her. Kneeling by her coffin, he
kissed her.

Snow White sat up, blinked, and smiled. The
Prince's kiss had broken the evil spell!

As the Dwarfs danced with joy, the Prince
carried Snow White off to his castle, where they
lived happily ever after.